COWBOY RODEO

**Written and Illustrated
by JAMES RICE**

PELICAN PUBLISHING COMPANY

GRETNA 1992

The word "Pelican" and the depiction of a pelican are trademarks of Pelican Publishing Company, Inc., and are registered in the U.S. Patent and Trademark Office.

Library of Congress Cataloging-in-Publication Data

Rice, James, 1934-
  Cowboy rodeo / written and illustrated by James Rice.
    p.   cm.
  Summary: Describes the atmosphere and the events of the
rodeo in its early days.
  ISBN 0-88289-903-1
    1. Rodeos--United States--History--Juvenile literature.
2. Frontier and pioneer life--West (U.S.)--Juvenile
literature. [1. Rodeos--History. 2. West (U.S.)--Social
life and customs. 3. Frontier and pioneer life--West
(U.S.)] I. Title.
GV1834.5.R53 1992
791.814'0973--dc20   91-34924
                                                          CIP
                                                           AC

Printed in Hong Kong
Published by Pelican Publishing Company, Inc.
1101 Monroe Street, Gretna, Louisiana 70053

Rodeo got its start in the days of roundups and big cattle drives. It grew out of the cowboy's occupation.

Texas Jack sez thar warn't much money in the Southwest then, jus' a few million cows runnin' loose and free for the taking, but no local market.

Ranch children grew up learning about cattle and the ways of the range. Everyone had special chores to do.

Texas Jack sez they had their own
meanings for the three Rs, namely—
ropin', ridin', and rasslin'.

At roundup time several neighboring ranchers
got together to collect the cattle into one herd
and brand the spring calves.

Texas Jack sez it wuz easy to tell who the suckin' calves belonged to, but last year's mavericks sometimes sparked some purty good arguments.

The horse wranglers had their jobs
cut out for them.

Texas Jack sez them wranglers wuz
a rough bunch.

The cook had to be first up at dawn and last down after dark, and he always had to have a pot of coffee going.

Texas Jack sez a good cook could shore make the trail seem shorter. If he wuz really bad, he might not see the trail's end.

The trail drive could last for months, but it seemed to last forever. Roping and riding and such came to be second nature.

Texas Jack sez if the cows went too fast they'd walk the fat off. A good trail boss could fatten a herd on the trail.

At trail's end cowboys from different outfits had to find out who had the best ropers and riders.

Texas Jack sez it wuz shore a good way for the cowboys to let off a little steam.

Each outfit had to test its string to see who had the fastest horses.

*Texas Jack sez the races were known
to spark a wager from time to time.*

If each outfit had a fast horse, it also had an especially mean horse.

Texas Jack sez ever' outfit had at least one raunchy ol' bronc and at least one cowboy that figgered he could stay on anything with four legs.

Roping was the basic skill of the cowboy and naturally they had to have a contest to see who could rope the fastest.

Texas Jack sez some cowboys could rope a calf and pin it down almost before he could get good off his horse.

Some contests didn't have anything to do with cowboy skills—a cowboy just wanted to show how tough he was.

Bill Pickett, a black cowboy, was the first to jump off a galloping horse and tackle a running steer.

Texas Jack sez that's how bulldoggin' came about.

One day some unknown cowboy, half crazy and all tough, straddled a wild bull and a new contest was started.

Texas Jack sez the bull is the only bucking stock that sets out to get the cowboy. The cowboy ain't safe till he's out of the arena. Now they've added clowns to protect the cowboy.

Women raced a pattern around three barrels without knocking any over.

Texas Jack sez he figgers the men wuz afraid they might come out second best if they had to run against some of them fast gals.

Later, women competed in the rough riding events, with different rules. They could hold on with both hands and the time was shorter.

Bareback riding was the latest rough riding event added to the contest. There's no saddle, only a handhold, and the rider has to spur all the way.

Texas Jack sez it izn't the most dangerous, but it's prob'ly the hardest ridin' event as far as staying on 'cause thar jus' ain't enough to hang on to.

COWBOY RODEO

Texas Jack sez a real high roller could purt' near jar a body's teeth loose.